Terre Haute
—Stories—

Mike Beal

RoseDog🐾Books
PITTSBURGH, PENNSYLVANIA 15238

RoseDog Books
585 Alpha Drive, Suite 103
Pittsburgh, PA 15238
Visit our website at *www.rosedogbookstore.com*

ISBN: 978-1-64957-896-9
eISBN: 978-1-64957-917-1

Contents

Introduction

I'd put it off for so long it was almost comical, finally now at 32 getting pressure from both parents to do something with my life, stop living at home and working low-wage cooking jobs.

So without the long-term hope of any financial stability or even any assured success of any other kind, I applied for a teaching assistantship at Indiana State from my home computer at my home in my not-so-homey hometown of South Bend, and much to my shock, got approved for it.

I'd grown up in South Bend, fetched a BA in English from IU Bloomington, and then lived in various places like Colorado, Indianapolis and Washington D.C. South Bend, though plagued by violent crime and economic squalor, is still very morally indignant in its own way, populated substantially by the religious right. They took exception apparently to my marijuana conviction of 2006 (it's 2016 by the time I'm applying for this assistantship) and deemed me unfit for teaching secondary school, for substitute teaching, and actually even substitute bus driving.

There were things I liked about my hometown — it's substantially bigger than Terre Haute and sometimes when you're walking around downtown at night, or on the near East side, you can just HEAR this humming that's like this mathematical consummate of all these seemingly unrelated industrial machines, just singing their own ambient song into the night. There are electric lights on nondescript buildings, buildings which in their anonymous blankness seem like models of humility and unquestioning functionality.

But it was a mini-South Side, all the way. I'd be riding my bike around on some nights, even right downtown, and I'd just get this creeping feeling like I better not ride down this block because there's a mugger or murderer waiting to nab my $15. There was a murder the last summer I lived there, at night, right across the street from the bar I worked at. My bar was sort of seedy but sat right next door to this pretty swanky Irish pub that serves boxties, and whatnot.

And something was pushing me out of my hometown, as usual. It's a place that's good at that sort of thing, whether it's a dude you work with who just seems like he sniffs glue, or a library cop giving you the stare down like you just stomped on his gerbils with golf cleats, or a fat dude who thinks he's Johnny Depp rubbing his body with a poker face on. The correct thing to do to South Bend is to leave it. It's similar to Detroit in this regard.

I scored an apartment down in Terre Haute and went ahead and signed the lease, without even visiting it. I'd never even been to Terre Haute before actually, other than driving through it on the way to Bloomington. It seemed kind of pretty, actually.

Chapter 1
Getting There, Getting Settled and Getting Planted

I got the key from my landlord and started moving in. Being from South Bend, I looked down my block and didn't really notice the busted out windows of the cars, the restraining order notices on the houses or the overgrown grass and weeds. It was like wallpaper to me... it was a background.

I got all my stuff out, among which was my bike, and I was carless, so my first Kroger run was destined to be pedaled to. On the way back, I had a bunch of stuff in my backpack and other provisions in bags that were suspended by a handlebar.

Riding down the main drag of the East side, which is Wabash Ave., I came to what must have been 19th or so. There was a truck waiting at the stop sign, I think a pickup, but I had the right of way, and assuming he'd seen me kept proceeding down Wabash, to the next reincarnation of the sidewalk.

But all of a sudden... WHAM! The pickup truck had started accelerating into its left turn, not seeing me riding, sending me off the bike and bending the front wheel. Also, you won't believe me, but I had eggs in that handlebar bag and NONE of them broke. I took that entire dozen eggs home and ate every one.

And the guy was cool as hell: but I fast got the impression that this town wasn't quite as bike friendly as my place of origin (which in turn probably isn't known for its bike friendliness itself). He got out, this fat Mexican on a 90-degree, humid day in August, was profusely apologetic and even somehow fixed my bike by stomping on the wheel until it was back into shape.

A little rattled, I got back on and rode it all the way home, drenched in sweat from the midday Terre Haute sun. I had to get ready for my mom and her boyfriend coming down with some of my stuff and cramming their faces with some food I cooked. And hell I still wasn't about to buy a bike helmet. Screw that.

Chapter 2
My Gas Station Orphan Vixen

Well, I'd got pretty settled in — got my teaching assignment (one class of ENG 101), books for my three grad classes, and my part-time job cooking at the Copper Bar, so I could ya know pay my rent and stuff. They gave me the day shift one Saturday instead of an evening shift, so that opened up that night, in early September 2016, for me to do whatever I wanted. I thought, well, I'm in Terre Haute, I might as well put on a wife beater and a Michigan hat and go out drinking and watching football.

I googled "sports bars." Later on, I'd come to find out, being presently puzzled at seeing "T.G.I. Friday's" pop up under said search, that Terre Haute's Friday's has one particularly becoming quirk about it: they bend the corporate rules by offering a full craft beer menu, something like 20 different local favorites from IPA's to stouts and back, instead of just doling out the usual eight options of things like Sam Adams and Heineken.

Sure enough, I went out, had a great time, got some sweet smiles from girls while riding my bike in my wife beater both on the way there and within the restaurant too, and thought, damn, I'm wearing a wife beater and drinking and watching football in a bar. That's really what I was doing.

Anyway, something funny happened later that night, when I stopped in to a nearby gas station to get a couple strawberry donuts and a can of mint Grizzly. Well, the clerk told me "Those donuts are terrible," first of all, which was kinda weird, especially since they were actually really tasty.

But anyway, there was this bird in front of me in line, real cute, talking about her mom for some reason, and she was like, "Yeah, I'm 22 and my mom's 38, she must have been like, 14 when she had me, or 16, or 20, Hell, I dunno!"

So there it was. I was witnessing new ground being broken in academic mathematics and child development, right before my very eyes. Life seemed like a pretty simple expedition at this point.

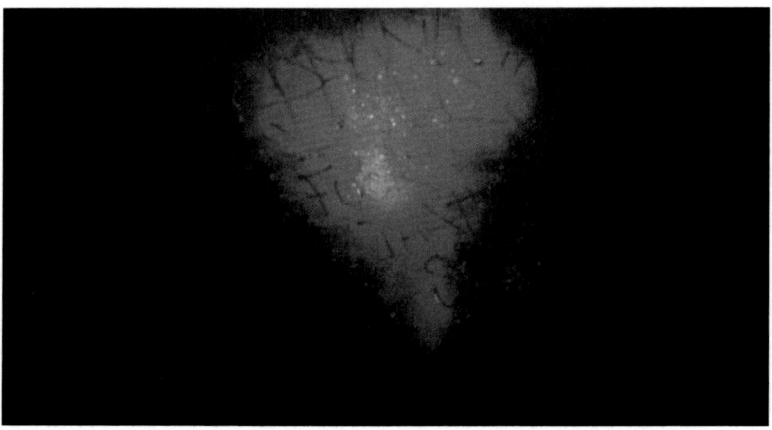

Chapter 3
Ruined for Life

Well, as I said, it had been a lot of riding my bike around looking for good places to get sh**faced at.

This "Show Me's" place was always kind of shrouded in mystery — they billed it as a "sports bar" but from the outside it looked more like a Spiece, the old sports apparel chain in northern Indiana that was the size of a warehouse and featured an indoor track for running around in, or a warehouse.

If you can believe it, the first time I went in Show Me's I didn't look at ANY of the girls working there, which is certainly weird in hindsight (at this juncture no gentlemen are employed on the front-of-house Show Me's team). I just went up to the TV's and noticed that they didn't have ANY of my games on so I just left for Friday's.

My next time in there I figured something's gotta be going on — it was my Indiana Hoosiers playing Iowa in the Big Ten Men's College Basketball tournament. Sure enough, the event was actually on the TV, but I got a surprise this time — this mouth-watering bartender dressed in a skimpy woman's t shirt and, basically, underwear, these spandex "shorts" which barely stretch down below the lower edge of the heiney.

My bartender reminded me of a snowflake — she was a brunette with this spooky beauty sort of like if you combined Snow White and the Wicked Witch of the West into one person, and she'd walk around with impeccable grace and smiles as she poured beers and answered questions. I'd later find out her name was Jess and I'd sort of half ask her out, to get a most polite and tactful declension, as I'm sure she's used to giving.

There was a more rotund redhead over there with a sort of mischievous face and dyed red hair, who came from Illinois on the other side from Terre Haute of the state border, but I just kept hitting on Jess, telling her she reminded me of a snowflake and that I loved the way she walked around. She was cool — even when I'd get too drunk to remember to pay, the next time she'd just docilely ask me to leave my credit card this time, and to be sure and fork over the cash.

Anyway, I basically couldn't stop going there. I'd lost my Show Me's virginity. This one time I literally had a religious experience looking at this girl's ass. It was like I saw in it the mystical essence of being 15 again and eating snacks, listening to music and playing video games in my friend's basement, which no, was not a sexual experience in its own right... we didn't quite swing like that.

But they like it — that's the thing. Some of them really have fun in there, in those skimpy uniforms, talking to each other, talking to us bar patrons, strutting their stuff and enjoying the lively, sporty atmosphere. And some of them are really smart, too, and funny — those were the ones I was really glad to see get out of there, if only for having the relief of never having to look at their little mountains and valleys of transcendence anymore, and also wanting something better for them.

Chapter 4

How to Stay on Task at Work, or Not and Say You Did

My coworker and I at city grass cutting were parked in the Gator, not doing anything, because he'd parked it and started not doing anything. He was staring down at his phone, a sort of vague smile on his face. I was just sitting there still and silent, glad to be getting paid for doing it.

Dudes would drive by periodically in City of Terre Haute trucks and one guy in one of these trucks saw us two in our Gator, looking pretty idle and a bit too comfortable, for being on the clock.

"Hey!" he yelled. "Get to work!"

My coworker just kept looking down at his phone, not even making any acknowledgement of the guy who had just yelled, still with that goofy half smile.

I got a little anxious. I didn't really want to get in trouble, so I thought I'd try to make some conversation and make some amends for the situation.

"He probably thinks you're ordering a pizza," I remarked.

A slight silence ensued.

After about 10 seconds or so, he simply presented to me nothing but the frank, direct interrogative: "How do you spell 'Hacienda'?"

Chapter 5

It's Probably Safe to Say I Fucked with the Wrong Redneck

I know up to this point in this book I've been a sarcastic wise guy, acting like my life is some sort of amusing board game of seeking lowbrow thrills and exhibiting a cursory, surface-level understanding of humanity. Well, this other night, while I was walking home from work at 7th & Elm, I got acquainted a little too closely with humanity and a little truth about the people in this town, which is that you probably shouldn't fuck with them, if you can avoid it.

But then, Terre Haute in a way is pretty similar to my hometown, South Bend, which I guess is a lot of where I originally got my confrontational nature at. It's run-down and depleted and it's frustrating too at the same time because a lot of the cultural developments that manifest themselves are these insipid, least-common-denominator products of overall corporate American zeitgeist of blank, generic uniformity, whether it's clothes from the mall dominating people's wardrobes or simplistic radio rock flooding people's radios and playlists.

The whole thing can really crank me out sometimes and on this particular night, I had a sort of crotchety mood about me where I felt like either smarting off to some loud mouth on the street or generally poking the vitriolic ball of homo sapien-ism I seemed faced with every day and which seemed poised for doing the same thing back, at any time.

I came to this one crosswalk on my way home. It was dark out, about 10:30 at night, six degrees outside with snow cover, I think a Wednesday night (I do remember it was Jan. 1, 2018).

Now, I'm somebody with really big feet, for whatever reason. I'm not sure if this comes into play in this story but anyway, this car stopped at the stop sign and I thought it was letting me go, so I waved and started walking. All of a sudden the car zoomed across the street and past me, right in front of me. You don't let shit like this ride where I'm from, so I gave the car a kick with my size 14 Skechers work shoes, which tend to be like the approximate texture of stone on the bottom.

Whoa, wrong thing to do.

This dude was full of mama's biscuits and gravy and probably a lot of rejection and frustration at living in a total shit town and he pulled his car over and got out.

"Did you just kick my car?" he yelled.

"Yeah!" I said, back, just normal.

I heard him yelling like "fcking mther fcker" or something along those lines and then saw him going to his trunk.

And he had a baseball bat.

Now, the ground was like covered in ice: the chances of me not tearing an ACL if I tried to run were almost nil. Plus, I thought if I tried to run then he'd know where I lived and it would make him even more psycho, like when you run away from a dog. And he had a car and I didn't. I figured I'd try to talk it out with him.

Anyway I was walking away gingerly, having seen the bat, and he pulled up beside me and basically ran straight at me with it, in this big field by this store that I think sold meth out the back or something (which was closed now since it was night).

I tried to say, "Dude, chill out," to him, and sort of fell to the ground, trying to just deflect any blows he might give me and hopefully cool him down.

I figured all I did was lightly kick his car: it's not like I hauled off and roundhoused it or screwed his girl or something. He would probably chill out.

And ultimately I was right: not too much came from it, although it was so cold out that I didn't even realize at the time that he landed a couple blows just on my thighs, which I kind of had sticking in the air (I'm pretty sure it was so cold that my, uh, jewels were pretty much receded up into my pelvis, luckily enough), lumps that I'd notice later in the shower in the form of yellow, softball sized bruises on the backs of my upper legs.

He eventually simmered down (kind of) and drove away, but not before cussing the shit out of me some more and damn near knocking my front teeth out (which are false teeth in the first place) with some straight-ahead jabs of the bat. Also, he made me call myself a bitch. It's like, ok, dude. You've got the bat. But I was getting a taste of the locals… that's for sure. They didn't always fight fair and sometimes there was no defeating them on their home turf. It took wits and foresight just to satiate them.

I walked the two blocks back to my 62-degree apartment, got under some blankets and cracked a beer. At that point I think I was still regularly drinking decent beer, like Sam Adams, a luxury which was definitely not to last long.

Chapter 6

Sometimes in Life Your Bartender
is a Hot Crackhead from Idaho

Believe it or not, my next story comes from a night when it was six or so degrees out, too, and icy, early January. Indeed, the weather in Terre Haute is something that's almost like charming for its strident, unimaginable awfulness — there are very few places in the country hotter than that little pocket with Champaign and St. Louis in the summer, giving way then to winters that could get Sub Zero from Mortal Kombat saying "Fuck this."

I was on winter break from school/teaching, the winter before what I just related in the last story, working like a dog cooking at The Copper Bar as I had been since before the school year started, all throughout, as a measure toward payment of rent.

I got off work and was all ready to go home and chill, somehow to miraculously find something to do without cable, but they OFFERED you free beer after your shift. And I mean come on. I can't be that guy that turns down free beer.

So I PAINSTAKINGLY abided their policy, sat down at the bar and got served a cold, frothy tall IPA of some sort (yeah they don't just slap you a dusty can of Hamm's, as you can see).

There were two girls sitting down at the end of the bar, both of whom worked there. Some of the girls there took an interest in me, much to my excitement, or inertiac nausea, to be more exact (I'd actually achieved a noticeably and irksome bulge, irksome to the other party involved, that is, within my knicker garments, on my third or so day there when this girl was talking and smiling at me two feet away, squared up to my body and looking like Natalie Portman with an ass, Natalie Portman being my exact celebrity crush). It might have been my South Bend accent (bear with me), or the fact that I was a professor. I was bald, though, and had a shitty jawline from chewing so much tobacco.

But anyway sometimes things in life just fall into your lap, like my opportunity to get out of South Bend at all, in the first place did. But they were sitting down there and they were way more sociable than the girls back home, this one blond sometimes just spitting words at me with her acid-tinged left brain that I didn't mind at all, and the brunette kind of quiet and bitchy but with a porn star body.

Somehow they got talking to me.

"Your name's Mike right?"

"Yes it is," I said back, in a sort of wise-guy, game show host tone, which I figured would go over well.

There was a little bit of small talk about how they'd thought they'd mistaken my name. Keep in mind, it was six degrees out on about January 4th (the year before my prior story), or four degrees on January 6th, the numbers get jumbled… but they struck me as just wanting something to do and not to sound like a good ol' boy but it just meant a little more to me than to them. I figured, if I keeping talking with these girls as the only worthy guy in the bar who's not working, there's no telling what will happen, and my life might be changed forever. I might start, like, wearing clothes from the mall, and shit. And I didn't want to do that, unless we're talking about sports jerseys or Soundgarden t shirts.

So with a heart rate surely over 100, anyway, I got out of there, remembering to say goodbye to them. I'm shy. That's what I do. I go home and listen to music.

But you know when you START drinking and you just don't want to stop? That free beer after work crap ended up costing me more money than it saved me, hands down.

But I just had to stop in Ripley's, this bar right on the way home.

The bartender here was pretty cute — a little portly but a handsome-faced brunette. But boy were her eyes wild!

I remember her talking fast, about the other bars she worked at, looking at me with big, moist and polymorphous eyes and a stone, expressionless face.

All the while, with no expression on her face, she'd take a liking to me more and more (some women favor my high forehead, or the fact that I'm a pretty copasetic bar patron when they're working, more likely), hooking me up with a couple free beers and periodically asking if I wanted to "go smoke with" her.

The thing is, she'd ask me that like every 15 minutes, and later I'd read online that that's exactly what crackheads do —

go smoke every 15 or so minutes and try to play it off like it's just cigarettes. Actually, I think I got so blacked out drunk that I did indeed go and freebase crack with her at some point, because I felt weird as hell the next day and hadn't touched any hard liquor, at least that I remember.

So this girl would just grab my pitcher when it was half full and fill it to the brim, not charging me for any of it, set it back down in front of me and keep talking to me, at one point offering to drive me back to her home of Idaho sometime, if I wanted. Luckily I was 33 and so, though still pretty adventurous, I'd learned from experience and from Lou Reed both to "Don't believe half of what you see / And none of what you hear".

Anyway, the last thing I remember from that night, other than this grizzly ex-con bastard yelling "You got a nice ass" at her (it was decent... a little wide and definitely not like Natalie Portman at The Copper Bar), was her sitting down in a bar stool at the end of the bar and me giving her a back rub, hehe. Silly times. I just wish I remembered what happened after that. I think.

Chapter 7

You Might Be an Alcoholic if…

When you're a TA at a university, "free time" is basically a figment of your imagination. For my part, in particular, I'd spent much of the school year teaching, taking a full graduate course load and also working 20-30 hours a week on the side as a cook to pay my rent, so I was in an especially feeble position to foster any hobbies or outside pastimes.

The time came around late January where my course work mounted and I had to quit my side job. I took to donating plasma, a process which I think came close to killing me one time because I drank coffee that morning absentminded of their precaution not to, as well as inadvertently garnering some sympathy money out of my mom in the form of $200 here and there. And I discovered I could pay my rent with my credit card — a great concept until your ass is neckhigh in debt and toiling feverishly just to pay off the interest, the beast of principal lurking down there with malevolent eyes.

But all that was a matter for a different time — now it was time to bang out this 16-page paper on Invisible Man [1], or spend 12 or so hours on a Saturday doing research, more accurately. And for graduate students in English, much of the research simply involves what KIND of research you want to shift to later, when you get to the nuts and bolts of your paper amassing.

So I concluded by work about 10 pm for the day, on a Saturday, having barreled away at it nonstop since I got out of the shower and got some breakfast in me, and I decided to check my email. And it was some bullshit semantics from my dad about something that had happened in our family close to 20 years prior, something I hardly had the patience to deal with at the moment.

And so I thought, this is enough. I'm going out. I'm so done with this day.

I went to the college bar and had a great time but they closed at 2 and I figured hell, I'm not done with my night yet. I didn't go to IU to learn to stop partying at 2.

The only bar still open on my way home was actually the place I'd worked at, which I sometimes liked to avoid because it often contained the sort of "upper crust" [2] of Terre Haute, people who rubbed shoulders with the opulent owner who also purveyed the Indiana Theater [3] and whatnot. But going home probably would have led to a crazed homicide of (myself) by (myself), by way of some sort of phenomenological self-dissociation and extreme frustration.

Hell, it wasn't even frustration. It was like disgust with the world. I had no free time, I was a complete slave to my job and it paid $440 per two-week pay check. And the work was only going to get more daunting from here. To be honest, I'm the type of person to have a lot of hobbies — I'm a blogger, I paint, write poetry, fiction short and long, and enjoy exercising as well as playing and watching sports. This grad school life was bogging me down to the point where I really felt like lashing out at the world — plus my dad was pissing me off with that annoying email.

So I went into the bar and honest to God I was having a great time and wasn't being a problem at all — I was shooting the shit with my guy I'd used to cook with in there, who'd just got off his shift, and was even getting great vibes from all the bartenders.

Over in the corner there was this waitress standing there who I swear was like ALWAYS there — she'd been there the night I'd been in there before I went and saw that crack bitch, and she was always standing over in the corner. To be honest, I don't think she really approved of me — I probably stared at her bust too often when I worked with her and she probably was of the opinion that I went there and drank too much in my spare time. She was certainly something sort of resembling Terre Haute's rogue sociological elite, although there were definitely better looking girls than her in town.

Well for what I think is a reason somewhere along these lines, I was the victim on this night of what I personally think was an ambush, in the form of this cop noticing me pissing in the girls' restroom. Now, you might say that sounds disgusting, but I had many reasons for doing it — there was no one in there, when I entered or exited (not that I could see into the future or anything), it was 2:30 in the morning, the guys' was full of these douche bags doing their hair, and… I really had to piss, the way only drunks truly know.

Well this cop started jawing at me, telling me I had to leave and that they'd thrown out my beer. Now, I actually had a history of going psycho when people touched my beer — truth be told I'm a pretty docile dude but there's times in my life where it's a good thing I don't own an AK-47.

So I stood there arguing, saying no way in hell am I leaving and pour me a new beer, and finally they pushed me out. So we were out on the sidewalk in February and I'm all ready to come to blows, or I think I am, so I yelled "I'm gonna beat your ass" at the cop like only the most clownish drunk would do (this was an excellent lesson in never getting a fight with a cop, all in all) and started charging at him, only to have my arm grabbed in pursuit by his partner, and thrust back and snapped, just like that, the bone fractured and all. The next thing I know I'm slammed down on my face (somehow my nose didn't get broken but just scuffed… that must be where all my calcium flows to or something), with broken arm and now wrist too, getting handcuffed.

I'd been so drunk that five or so hours later, when they woke me up in the drunk tank, I didn't remember everything that had happened and I guess couldn't feel all my broken extremities, so I figured they were getting me up to send me out on my way with a citation and a future court date.

"Nope," said the guard. "You tried to attack the cop. You're coming with me."

And he led me to the Division 6 detainment room. All of a sudden it didn't look like I'd be teaching the next day.

[1] For what it's worth this Ralph Ellison novel is probably one of the best of the 20th century.

[2] It's hard to explain but Terre Haute is ostensibly flooded with what I'd like to refer to as a very esoteric aristocracy with a proclivity to do things like sending you a fake $600 water bill (which yes actually happened to me on multiple occasions and among other similar devious permutations), listing any amount of legal speak but conspicuously missing an actual NUMBER next to the words "case number." I'm not kidding. There would be the words "case number" and then a period. One hand washes the other… yeah, if you're a sucker, that is.

[3] The Indiana Theater was a venue that housed things like country music concerts, Rosanne Bahr comedy routines and such.

Chapter 8
Jail

With my buzz slowly but steadily wearing off, I was led into a room about the size of an elementary school classroom full of inmates, all dudes (all of whom I think were actually white, which is and was sort of puzzling) dressed in orange shirts and pants, in which I was likewise presently garbed. I was pretty much frozen stiff in a state of petrified mania and I'm sure the guys picked up on this, a fact probably correlative with the fact that I ended up getting along pretty decently with just about everyone. Actually, I got through my whole time in the joint without any altercations, which wasn't always the case with my drunk tank stints in college.

There were a couple "hey"'s from a couple dudes, there was a 15-or-so-inch TV on a wheeled stand playing some cable movie, and on two sides of the room was a dark glass in which we saw our reflections.

It was Sunday and the spirit of the Sabbath must have been rampant throughout the premises because the mood and

atmosphere seemed just amazingly light and jovial to me —
then again I was from South Bend, a backdrop against which
most things on the planet seem light and jovial, by comparison.
There were board games, chatter from almost all both earnest
and mocking, and a couple dudes walking back and forth across
the room repeatedly, just for something to do.

I got introduced to my bed situation at some point, which
was in a room with about five or seven other mattresses, some
on top bunks, lower bunks or "floor," the latter of which was
my charming sleeping level. Much of the ensuing time ended
up centering itself on this room, entailing activities of just nap-
ping, lying and staring at the ceiling, or sharing jokes and
stories with the other inmates. One of the dudes was from Mus-
kegeon, Michigan, a town I didn't know too much about other
than that I'd heard it was actually worse than South Bend,
which seemed like a paradigmatic impossibility to me. He had
a story about going into a house full of black dudes with a gun
and getting some money from them, followed by the self-ag-
grandizing quip "Now that's some gangster shit," and he had
this funny term for the meat loaf they served us at lunch, "Cat-
head." A couple 40-something dudes were cool and would tell
stories and jokes. If I'd been blind to my surroundings and
clothing, I might have thought I was at work cutting grass or
welding steel.

One dude was in for arson, six years, was undersized and
had this funny, slow and high-pitched way of talking. He
seemed honest, all in all.

Oh come to think of it there was ONE black dude in there,
with dread-locks. We both agreed that smoking weed sucked

and we liked getting wasted on alcohol. Somehow he got to joking about how he wanted to fuck a college chick and give her AIDS and that's about when I stopped talking to him. But he was pretty cool, overall.

I got this one sort of death glare from this shaved-head dude, a predicament which has also plagued my own dome since I was about 22. Other than that, I had a great time. Ok, that's an exaggeration. But it wasn't the constant rapes and knife-fights I'd envisioned when I first walked in there, so that was good. I even caught one (uneventful, thankfully) hot shower while I was in there for the 54 hours or so, in full view of the entire room but with about a three-foot cement rampart before me. Not bad. Like being in high school gym class again.

They sent this college girl in on the first day to lead me up for an x-ray and it's terrible, but I got physically aroused, almost right when I looked at her. I'm not sure if it was just the release of being around all those guys and then seeing this young, shapely sanctuary of femaleness gazing at me with a vague smile, smooth face and these watery, innocent eyes, but something got triggered in me and the thing just wouldn't settle down. I still had this cumbersome bulge in my loose orange pants, actually, which had boxers under them, when I went up to get the x-ray which I think they rushed through and tabbed as "negative" despite the fact that I literally couldn't move my arm and would be trying to grab my meal tray and cup of Kool-Aid with one hand, dropping them all over the place and shit.

My luck withstanding, it was President's Day weekend when I got locked up, so I was in for two whole days instead of one. But Tuesday morning came and a guard entered the bedroom at about 6 am and yanked my virgin ass out of there. To this day I have no idea how I avoided a coffee withdrawal headache all that time. I walked out, in the same clothes I'd had on that Saturday night, went to Walgreens and got some cinnamon rolls and a newspaper, went home, found my drugstore sling in my closet and put it on, set some coffee on the machine and started on my literary theory paper, all the while knowing I was pretty much fucked. I'd had to call off of teaching from a jail room telephone, the day prior.

Chapter 9
Dogs, Dogs, Dogs

It certainly was nice have my freedom back — to be able to wander the streets as I saw fit, any direction I liked, whenever I felt like it. Unfortunately, there were many times I wished I couldn't say the same for our canine friends.

So yeah, dogs. I guess these are things that a lot of people like. It's something I've come to grips with over the course of my life. People just like dogs. They get pleasure out of being around these creatures that are loud, drool, smell bad, chew things up, have to get "walked" every day, and are potentially lethal.

I mean ok yeah — they're kind of charming, I suppose. Growing up I always had a cat in the house but there was this one stint of about two days when we were taking care of a friend's gold lab in our house. And I have to admit, there was a sort of endearing quality about the way he'd sit next to me while I watched TV. It was like he didn't need anything and he enjoyed and even extolled my company and attention.

As you know, dogs come in many different "breeds," and one useful permutation of the animal in Terre Haute is definitely the "watchdog." Actually, after I got kicked out of my teaching assistantship (the official reason for which termination was grades, although I'd never really get a straight answer on why I was getting C+'es on papers), I worked with this dude from Rochester, New York, a town I don't usually think of as some white bread utopia. But Terre Haute even threw him for a loop — his house got burglarized within the first two weeks of him living there and suddenly it didn't seem so weird that pretty much everyone and their mom seemed to own some giant, potentially murderous dog, the function of which all of a sudden probably went beyond "endearing soul mate," or whatever.

Um. Just don't walk around Terre Haute, Indiana. Just don't do it. Sure, it's three hours west on I-70 of Dayton, Ohio, where a dude was mauled to death in 2018 by a pit bull. Sure, it's five hours southeast of the Wisconsin town where this girl's own one-year-old Frenchie did her in because he'd been trained to fight by the previous owner.

But, sometimes even worse than dogs, Terre Haute is full of PEOPLE. And I don't mean to sound misanthropic (that shouldn't sound that misanthropic, I figure), but you know how people are. They do things like flood to crowded churches, bars and beaches in the throes of the coronavirus pandemic, and touch seven different packages of pork rinds while standing one foot behind you at the grocery store before finally (ideally) actually choosing one.

And they say things like, Oh, she's nice, she won't bite, when this giant half-boxer half-German shepherd is walking right behind you without a leash on in the middle of the day. It's like, gee, yeah. People are sure a reliable source of information, the same party that once informed us that cigarettes made you healthy and skinny.

It was funny — this time, on 6th between Park and Farrington, the same dog had run after this black dude and he literally hurdled this porch barrack of some nearby house, an obstruction that was almost as tall as him (sorry to reinforce a stereotype but that was definitely an exemplary instance of black Americans' superior athletic ability). But then the juices get flowing in your system sometimes and you're capable of extraordinary stuff — I pulled a similar move at Show Me's one time, trying to walk in and coming across this Boxer in the parking lot, who'd been out playing around the lot, terrorizing people, only to retreat into this row of bushes and then re-emerge RIGHT when I was trying to make my way toward the entrance. The fence I hopped was a solid five feet high and surrounded the bar's outdoor seating area, so you might say I made an unorthodox entrance into that establishment that day. But Terre Haute is the kind of place where something like this happens and nobody even bats an eyelash. And it's not like they're being smug or rude — they just actually realize that I'm another honest, hard-working dude and that I just had to flee for my life away from a giant dog.

Carrying a styrofoam box full of a Swiss burger and fries by this pair of canines that sat outside every day, without leashes on, could certainly be an adventure on certain days after work. Then there was this other day when I walked out of my apartment to go to my anger management class and I literally got "dogged out" — I called them up and told them I couldn't make it because there was a giant dog out on the sidewalk in front of my place, just roaming free.

But the scariest instance of all had to be the final incident I encountered that involved a potentially dangerous, tail-wagging little monster. I was walking back with my laundry pack, again down 6th Street which might have been kind of stupid, and at one point I passed the café on Washington and almost ran into this dude who I thought was dressed in obnoxiously trendy or corporate clothing, something that happened pretty often in that town. But I was nice to him anyway and said "Excuse me," or whatever, not noticing that he started taking the same route I was, right behind me.

I got about one block up and all of a sudden this pit bull started trotting toward me — not really running full speed, not foaming at the mouth or looking too maniacal or anything, but also not doing what I'd readily describe as "smiling," either. She was just a shark-toothed cur without a cause, you could say.

So I froze. I stood stone still. And then I started walking, very slowly, being careful not to make too sudden or startling of movements, across the street and in the opposite direction. And lo and behold, sure enough, she followed me, right across the street. So I decided to put down my pack — if I know dogs, they're usually stupid enough to be curious about every little object they come across, and sure enough, this bought me a second or two as she went over to my laundry bag and started sniffing at it. I think I climbed on top of the nearest car. Suddenly, though, there was that same dude, whom I'd almost run into outside the café, saying he thought she was "friendly" because she was wagging her tail, but saying he'd walk with me for a half block or so. I have to say this dude was badass, like I'm sure lots of people in that town are. I was shaking like a top, with no intention of looking cool or tough, just gimme my purse and get me the fuck back inside my apartment. Eventually, the dog sprinted back across the street to the side opposite us, making sure to dart right in front of a car and come within a foot of getting struck and killed, while she was at it.

But at the end of the day, I think dogs go about as people do. I mean, there are people you come across in lots of towns who could conceivably kill you, on the spot, and we have mechanisms for doing so more elaborate and less noble than simple dental incisors. That is, if people weren't so hell bent on robbing each other, there wouldn't be the need for all these pit bulls, Saint Bernards (though I lived next to a really cool Saint Bernard I have to say), Rottweilers and crap, and dogs would really be man's best friend. Gee, your best friend is a slobbering oaf that's not housebroken and will eat its own shit if you let it. Nothing pathetic about that or anything.

36 · Mike Beal

Chapter 10
The End of the World

I don't know that this matters, but I'm writing this on May 18.

Now, probably not a lot of you, but some of you, might already know what this "story" is about, just from its association with that particular date in May, which relates tangentially to my erstwhile locale of Terre Haute but mostly to America, to music, to rock, to drugs, to youth decaying into middle age and some wisdom from of all people Oasis, who once sang "Please don't put your life in the hands / Of a rock and roll band / And throw it all away".

Three years prior to the date I'm writing this, in the wee hours of the morning, Chris Cornell, lead singer of pioneering Seattle grunge band Soundgarden, fatally hung himself in his hotel room following a show in Detroit.

At the time, I was very much in a strange position in life, myself. Like I said, I'd lost my teaching assistantship, an event that occurred just a week or so earlier, and the reason was average grades. I'd chanced upon a summer job cutting grass for the City of Terre Haute and the physical, ambulatory nature of the job combined with the warm spring air was very good for me. It might have very well saved my own life.

I think I was still on the first week of that job when I came home and heard the news by way of social media, which I imagine is how most people heard the news, as especially un-"grunge" as that is. When I saw what had happened, I did what is often my knee-jerk reaction to any emotional cataclysm, or a comfort blanket, which was I started writing. I found that the words came from me easily, to the point where almost immediately, after putting together 400 commemorative words for my music blog Dolby Disaster, I decided to augment the project into a "12 Days of Soundgarden" series. I made the pact that for the next 12 days, a number I came up with for I suppose biblical reasons which is of course again very un-"grunge" I must admit, I wouldn't discuss anything on my blog other than the late singer's first band (I realize I'm leaving out Audioslave and his solo stuff and don't mean to disrespect any fans of that material) and if I could avoid it, I wouldn't even TALK about anything other than Soundgarden, 'til after Memorial Day. Needless to say, I'm not the type to say much or talk on the phone. I cooked all my meals at home and didn't really associate with society too much, since I'd stopped teaching, save for necessity.

Well, I certainly had one weakness, which I've already addressed, which would be the half-naked girls at Show Me's. I'm telling you: if you're a hormonally charged guy and experience seeing them for the first time, it's like nothing else you've ever come across. For the record, I've only been in a strip club twice in my life and it was to deliver a pizza, both times.

But I'd been at Show Me's the night before, May 17, 2017, and perhaps into the morning of May 18. And I barely remembered what had happened, but I smashed my bike, after coming out of the bar, because it wouldn't ride right. It was an old and shitty bike I'd got used, for the record. And to this day I have no idea how I got to or from work that day. I just remember getting home and seeing that news of what had happened, which had taken place just about the same time I for no reason, with no memorable anger in my system or impetus for doing at all, picked up my bike repeatedly outside the bar and smashed it against the ground, bending both wheels, then walking it home. Later that evening, it stood, mangled, insulted, debased and ruined, in my closet nook just outside of my living room. And it kind of made sense to me.

But life had to go on. I think I went out again that night (typically I didn't go out two nights in a row but it did happen from time to time). It was the end of the world to me but life had to go on. And what I mean is that my entire conception of reality was inverted. My exact beacon, my ideal of what is was to be "invincible," was defeated, forever. Actually, I'd shared "Black Hole Sun" when the unthinkable happened six months earlier in Donald Trump being elected president. This was the music I leant on when nothing else was working and when it seemed I couldn't go on, couldn't put on any type of passable face for the world, without it. As Bob Dylan would say, "Now everything's a little upside down / As a matter of fact the wheels have stopped / What's good is bad / What's bad is good". Or Everlast: "I've seen the good side of bad / And the down side of up / And everything between". In the end, I didn't miss any work and I eventually got over what had happened but how's this for poignant intervention: it was cloudy outside for the next 11 days in Terre Haute, the sun not emerging until the final, 12th day of my Soundgarden series, Memorial Day 2017. Now Terre Haute is a pretty weird place and I'm sure I'm forgetting something or another but the only other weird thing I remember specifically happening at this exact time was that the temperature reading on the Walgreens sign said it was -196 degrees outside. There was no doubt: Hell had frozen over.

[1] Please excuse my "Siamese dreamin'" here.

Chapter 11
You Stepped into the Wrong Dog Kennel, Sonny Boy!

Do you ever GO OUT?

Now, you'd think, with going out, it's a hazard best avoided... blah-betty-blah... and you do it when you're feeling your worst, with that bored, claustrophobic feeling sitting around staring at the same four walls in your apartment.

But sometimes I'm not so sure. Sometimes, it seems to me, I go out because I get this FEELING like it's going to be great. Actually, the strongest urge I ever got to I think was this one time when it got up to 60 degrees in January when I was just starting my spring semester at ISU. I sort of got on my bike and headed down to Friday's, half hating myself because I'd just hit up I think Tacos & Tequila the last night, but eventually finding this gorgeous Italian girl and having an hourlong conversation with me with her voluptuous mom sitting next to her, and this girl I'd worked with from before, tall, with straight blond hair and too luscious to even believe, resting her mystical, bright eyes on me for brief sessions.

Well there was this other night in February 2019 that was frigid cold, probably not over 10 degrees out, but I got the same feeling, so I decided to hit up an Irish pub I usually had a pretty decent time at. And I hadn't been out in like five or six days, I don't think.

Now, I feel it's important to preface what I'm about to say. There's an extent, that is, to which words are immaterial in describing certain things.

We're living in a curious confluence as we near the quarter mark of the 21st century. I don't think anyone would deny that. We're living in a time when the reality of the world moves fast and subsumes your mind like a tsunami, so that when you finally realize some overarching truth about it, you're liable to be driven to enraging anger at the mark of mania, or even slaughter of yourself and another.

We live in a world of copious, rampant killing, and violent crime, of boarded up buildings, of rampant pollution plaguing our lands and waterways, of globalism gone awry, in other words. And it's presented to us almost as if it's a spectacle, as if it's entertainment. And the way this works is that when somebody sees a problem in the world, they blame it on a politician. Politicians are sitting ducks before debased, frustrated, desperate consumers longing to have a good time for the purpose of rubbing it in to their cohorts that they had a good time.

It's all pretty hopeless, isn't it?

And then there were those pants. I haven't even gotten into that yet.

It's really awkward but the first two girls I ever saw wearing yoga pants in a place that wasn't the gym or Buffalo Wild

Wings were my two cousins, both of whom are like four years younger than me. And my heart just fell. I knew we'd been forsaken. Expelled from paradise. I can't believe them when they say that it's alright [1].

Djuwanna stand for something? No? You'd probably rather get laid, right? Yes?

Ever notice how the girls who get real mad that guys hook up with younger girls are like fat, or have unwanted facial hair?

Ok, I'm digressing here. But I'm trying to prove a point (and remember this was a bar so all the patrons had to be at least 21, since we're not in Bloomington anymore) here about the naturally precarious backbone of conviction, in human life. And I don't mean to jab at anybody who "stands up for something," whether it's a girl shaving her head into a Mohawk, a black person wearing a shirt with Marcus Garvey on it or that dude in the video store stabbing his co-worker for saying Return of the Jedi is better than The Empire Strikes back.

I'm not saying it doesn't happen and that would be repugnantly near-sighted of me to say that it doesn't at all. But I would like to cautiously hypothesize that it's usually desperation that drives people to lead these "semantic existences" or whatever and if a girl is really pretty, or a guy is really handsome, he or she is likely to want to be normal.

What's more, and you might never believe me, but THEY'RE TRYING TO BE NICE.

When people fit in, sure, it's for their own good, but maybe the way in which they're "fitting in," such as the clothes they're wearing or whatever, is just a way of saying it doesn't MATTER and they want to get on to things that are real in life, like laughter, kindness and respect.

Somewhere in the Pacific Northwest right now (not to be confused with the Atlantic Northwest) there's a person bitching. I know it. And I've never even been to the Northwest. But I know there's someone up there, wearing a shirt that says "Capitalist," who probably like doesn't BELIEVE in eating food, and shit, and they hate yoga pants, or maybe they actually hate yoga pants but they're claiming to like them because they think hating yoga pants is "played out." This person will die someday but not before watching lots of episodes of It's Always Sunny in Philadelphia. They will have the dimensions of Danny Devito's body memorized in their mind. And they fully deserve it. The organism morphs in toggling between rancorous, expletive tart and TV-borne blob.

So I was millions and millions miles from this type of thing, in Terre Haute, on this night. Terre Haute is not a place anybody would think to go for fun and it's hardly a place anybody would go out of necessity. But there I was, making the mile long or so walk to the pub from my apartment at 8th and Crawford, passing the giant mural of a Coca-Cola bottle on the side of the Coke museum thing or whatever, passing a Domino's Pizza (the only pizza on the planet I won't eat, as far as I know) and a Walgreens before getting to the pub.

I walked into the bar feeling perhaps unusually confident but low-key nonetheless. I glanced up at the clientele and I remember being greeted by these two sets of brown eyes. That was the first thing I saw. I saw four eyes.

The eyes were not so much FIXED on me as they GATH-ERED me, like gushing, rapturous waters from a tropical tsunami.

It was the clientele. I strolled past, doling a quick, congenial smile, sat two seats down at the bar and put on my Mr. Cool persona, like you do in middle school, or whatever.

Over in the corner, there was sitting the kitchen manager of the place. I knew he was the kitchen manager because he sat there every night, drinking for any number of hours, after he got off work, and one time he offered me a job as a shit-on line cook, despite the fact that I was already cooking 20-30 hours a week at a bar down the street, teaching Freshman Writing and taking a full load of grad classes all at once.

Ok so he was down there and I was just not making eye contact... actually he'd been too haughty to even say hi to me another time after that I'd been in despite the fact that he looked like someone who'd be on the show Cops and not have a uniform on, if you know what I mean. He looked like a Terre Haute resident, in other words. And if you think it's weird that this town is full of gangly looking dudes and women of magnanimous aesthetic splendor then sugar, you're a lot like me.

I'm not going to make this too long frankly just because I don't have the power to. Or I want to feel good again at some point in this day. Actually I'm up at 10 after eight in the morning writing this, maybe out of providence, in that regard.

Ok so the girls were two exorbitantly beautiful young ladies from some place called Jasper, which I only recognized from seeing their high school football team on the local news a couple times. One was blond and one was brunette. They both had long, straight hair. And they were both in yoga pants. I guess those things are weirdly fitted for winter though I heard some girls wear leggings under them.

And you'll never believe me. But these girls were NICE. They might have things called HEARTS. They might be what you'd classify as HUMAN BEINGS.

Well, something was driving them to go out on this night, to Terre Haute, which they likely considered a city, though it was a bumfuck dot on the map to me, evident from my constant infestation of its crime-addled middle portion.

And sometimes you do what you can but the overall circumstance is too dire for you to handle. That is, I feel bad, because I highly doubt that these girls had a good time this night. They deserved to. One thing I saw about them is that though they made eye contact with me they had the coolness to leave me alone. I liked them for this. And it wasn't like they were being rude. They were sitting there talking, perfectly friendly, in voices like whispering winds on rose petals, giving the bar exactly what it needed, which was simply, them.

I don't suppose I needed them. And it's a good thing. That is, when I finally did strike up conversation with them (I think we were talking about the West coincidentally but Cali instead of Portland or whatever) I happened to glance over in the corner and basically encounter the kitchen manager dude planting this glare on me as if he didn't just want to kill me but maybe like kill me, take my corpse, run over it, and platoon one of my eyeballs to keep it in a jar by his bedside.

I got the fuck out of that bar. And I still don't feel ok about it, to this day. I've tried to make novelty out of it. But I just don't feel ok. And I don't know what else to say about it. It's just what happened. Eh, I'd forgot to wear my dog collar, anyway, so maybe it was for the better.

"[1] Please excuse my 'Siamese Dreamin'' here."

Conclusion

Well, my friends, I can take a hint: this tried and true format of blabbering about my personal life in a little shithole town that isn't even my hometown is wearing a little thin. Who'd have thought that would ever happen?

I'm going to try to tie things up in a way that makes sense and maybe gives the reader some perspective on places like this. The long and short of it is that I eventually just ran out of money, making $9.50 an hour at my line cook job, not being able to find a better gig or a second job, and most of all, expecting my realtor to give me more than two days' notice before they came, changed the locks and repo'd all my shit (I was thinking more like 30 or 60 days... off by just a hair there).

There are a couple other pretty demoralizing things that happened (the stuff that usually holds decent entertainment value, I've found), like this car full of black kids pulling up to me and asking if I was Aryan Nation when I was walking back from work with my shaved head on a SULTRY night, or getting jumped coming out of Charlie's after having had a few choice words for this dude in there I'd worked with and who'd attempted to befriend me again, a dude who was there with a friend when I was alone.

The latter is kind of hard to talk about because my memory of it is basically non-existent but the strangest thing of all that happened is that on my last night in town, I was at The Verve and this cute, fiery little redhead girl started kissing me and letting me fondle her.

It goes like this.

I found out late that Friday night that I had to be out of my place by 9 am on Monday, or they were coming to change the locks, take away all my belongings and like piss on the floor, or whatever. That Saturday, early afternoon, I had to call my mom and tell her the news, and basically implicitly beg for a bed and a room to stay in, for the foreseeable future, while I basically had no job prospects. As has happened multiple times, she was compliant and affable to the point where it almost broke my heart and I almost started crying.

It was the ultimate gut check. One thing this girl said to me, during our spirited tonsil hockey match in The Verve, was "You seem humble." Well, I'd told her what had happened. How could I not be?

She was this buxom girl four years younger than me (so 32) named Kim who worked at the hospital and sang, or rapped, "Loser" by Beck, at The Verve's karaoke night that Sunday night. In a weird coincidence, my dad actually had his own affinity for Beck's schizophrenic rock-rap hit of the early '90s, even going so far as to purchase the CD single, which was full of some REALLY weird songs. He would pass away of a heart attack a mere month and a half after this event, on an unrelated note. But it's funny how sometimes something as strange and unlikely as "Loser" can sort of take the forefront in your life and act as a sort of center of your being — I guess it's proof that '90s music accomplished something after all, at least I hope.

I'll spare you too many of the details but suffice it to say we clicked, had both gone to IU for undergrad and loved music, also each hating Beck's album *Midnite Vultures*, and she was easy and great to talk to.

At one point, I'd told her I was moving back home the next morning (I definitely had no business getting that shlockered that night but I did anyway) and she responded with, "No, you're coming home with me!" Now, this was very flattering, having a girl say you could live with her and be her live-in fuck-buddy, more or less, but at the same time, I'm not stupid. I knew it was the alcohol talking, the same thing that told her going up and rapping "Loser" would be a good idea. Hell, I'd done that before, promised things to people when I was drunk only to recall it later and thank Christ that they hadn't actually been stupid enough to accept it.

But bars are a fantasy world. Let's be honest. It's the same way everywhere. They're where you go to escape reality and so for that reason, what happens in there tends to stay in there. There have been a couple of other times I've met girls in bars and to be honest it's never led to anything that good — the exact motive precipitating their going into that dark room to drown their sorrows in toxic swill isn't going to be thwarted by a little inebriated well-wishing and the root of the problem re-mains. Still, I hope this will provide a bookend to my Terre

Haute stories that stands as a little more uplifting than most of the rest of the content. Hell, it couldn't get much LESS uplifting. In finality, I declined Kim's offer to "get in this cab and do it," partly because I'm not going to do that to some poor cabbie, and partly because at 36, I'm square enough to take a good night's sleep, or a good three hours' sleep, in this case, over sex. I woke up the next morning, scurried completely out of my apartment with all my things by around 9:06, had the bizarre and unspeakable death of Kobe Bryant from the day before shift in and out of my head, got on the road, put in *The Best of Peter Tosh* and let "(You Gotta Walk and) Don't Look back" be my new mantra, an exceedingly welcome one if there ever were such a thing. But lemme tell you: I missed that girl SO bad the next three days. It was like I'd caught a "Kim bug," as I came to label it, that stayed with me a couple days just like the flu would. Hey, at least if we fail at everything else, men and women will always succeed in making each other miserable, I figure.